Neighbor Needed

Only the Exceptional Need Apply

TERESA WHITAKER

Tequan Books
Brooklyn, New York

ISBN: 978-1-7339148-3-3

Second book in this series:

Neighbor Needed 2

David's Song

In loving memory of Darryl, and for our son, Tequan.

Table of Contents

Chapter 1

Tasha Clarkson's parents had just purchased a new one-family house in an affluent neighborhood in Queens, New York, with a portion of their retirement monies. Now, Tasha Clarkson was their youngest child and the only one of their children still living at home in the downstairs apartment of their two-family brick home in Brooklyn, New York. Therefore, the parents gave Tasha the job of superintendent and landlord of the Brooklyn home. The Clarksons wanted their daughter to rent out their old top-floor apartment. They would split the rent accumulated from the rental in half. One part of the money would be for Tasha's parents as an extra income. They would give the other part to Tasha to pay the oil bill, insurance, and the taxes to maintain the Brooklyn home. They paid anything extra after those bills to Tasha for additional income to use in any way she pleased.

Tasha, who was a teacher in the city's public-school system, thought she could easily find a colleague who might be interested in renting the apartment. However, at the same time Tasha's parents were looking for a tenant to rent the second-floor apartment and they were not about to let just anyone live upstairs from their baby girl. Of course, they worried about Tasha's safety and wellbeing. This agreement would leave her alone in Brooklyn while the rest of her immediate family members and their spouses were all now living in Queens. However, for Tasha, who was extremely independent and maybe just a little overconfident, this was a challenge she believed she could handle on her own.

Tasha quickly started brainstorming ideas about how she could attract the best tenant for the rental. Creating a poster detailing all the perks of living in the area, including a detailed description of the apartment's layout, was first on her to do list. The next Monday morning, she planned to ask the principal if she could post a copy of her poster in the teachers' lounge. If not, she would give a few copies to her colleagues after brief conversations throughout the day. If no one at her school needed an apartment, they could pass the poster on to a friend or family member who might just be looking for an apartment. This way she could rule out the chance of renting the apartment to a psychopath. After working for an hour on the flyer, she settled down to have some dinner.

Later, Tasha figured she could grade a few test papers, take a long bath, read a delightful book, and doze off as she always did on a Friday night. While soaking in her tub, her mind wandered. Videos of past relationships started replaying in her head. She questioned whether she would ever find someone to settle down with. Her parents' relationship was admirable. However, Tasha could never seem to find what she was looking for in a man. Her first impressions of the men she had dated were always fantastic, however, the princes always turned out to be frogs in the end.

For instance, there was Carl, the surgeon who seemed perfect in every way. He was handsome, intelligent, and chivalrous, but his job was too demanding. Tasha barely saw him in person because of his busy schedule. Carl always bought her expensive gifts and sent her roses to make up for all the times he could not be there, but those gifts could not replace his presence. One day she surprised him at work. She wanted to take him out for a quick meal. Once there, Tasha was told Carl was not even on call that day. She immediately dialed his cellphone number to see what his excuse would be this time.

He picked up his phone and stated, "I can only talk for a moment, baby. They need me for another surgery. I have to scrub again."

Tasha replied, "While you're scrubbing for the next surgery, make sure you scrub off your lies. Yes, I know you're lying because I'm at the hospital now. I was told you are not even on call today, so I'm ending my calls to you forever!"

Now, this was the guy who Tasha's parents thought was perfect for her. He had the perfect job, a terrific background, drove a stylish car, and owned two homes. If only he could have surgically replaced his lying tongue, he would have been the total package.

Tasha was tired of letting her guard down to men who were only willing to play the dating game. She wanted a mature relationship now. So, she was taking a hiatus from dating to focus on herself for a while. This was a much-needed break. Her goals now comprised of taking long walks on the weekends and reading all the books she had collected for her own pleasure reading, but never read because she was constantly grading papers or calling parents. The walks went on for miles as she cleared her mind of all the debris from her past relationships and the mental strain of her job. Little did Tasha know; she would walk away from one chapter of her life and walk straight towards a new chapter opening before her soon.

Chapter 2

This Saturday's walk in the park felt different, brighter, and lighter than other days. Maybe it was the brisk autumn air kissing her face as she dashed down the paths, or it could have been the brightly colored leaves falling from the enormous trees on either side of the trail making her feel this way. Heaven knows what it was, but whatever it was, it was different.

The scenery was magical. Before she knew it, she was so lost in the moment's glamor; she bumped into a jogger headed toward her on the pathway. "Oh," Tasha said. While falling backwards a little, she felt two powerful arms grab her to stop her from tumbling to the ground. Wincing, she opened her eyes, becoming locked in a gaze with the handsome jogger.

"Are you okay?"

Those were the first words she heard him say.

"I'm fine," she replied shyly.

"Sorry, I should have been paying closer attention to where I was walking, but the trees are really beautiful this time of the year," Tasha explained.

"No problem," the stranger replied. "By the way, my name is David."

"I'm Tasha."

"Tasha, I'm new to the neighborhood and I normally like to go biking on weekends. Do you know anything about biking trails in the park, or biking in the neighborhood?"

"Well, I'm not a biker, but I've seen bikers on a bike trail out that way, north of here," Tasha replied.

"So, can I leave you with my number, Tasha? Maybe we can jog or walk the path together sometimes. I have recently landed a teaching job at the Carver School," David continued.

"I work at the Carver School," Tasha added.

"So, I guess we are going to be seeing a lot more of each other than we even expected," David stated excitedly.

"See you on Monday," Tasha said as she

waved goodbye.

Chapter 3

While moving their furnishings in to their new home in Queens, New York on Sunday morning, some neighbors who lived three houses down welcomed Mr. and Mrs. Clarkson to the neighborhood. The Johnsons were a lovely old couple. As the Clarksons and Johnsons chatted they talked about their children, rather they bragged.

"Will Tasha be moving in with you?" Mrs. Johnson inquired.

"No. Tasha wants to live close to her work site in Brooklyn, so she will be the superintendent and remain living in our Brooklyn property."

The Johnsons had two children: a daughter and a son. The son was the youngest and was still living at home. He had a scholarship to study law at Columbia University. He was just about to take the bar exam and join a law firm. Jerome Johnson was looking for an apartment in Manhattan, and his parents worried about where he would live. So, Mrs. Clarkson suggested Jerome look at the Brooklyn apartment since it was close to transportation and therefore easily accessible to Manhattan.

That night, the Johnsons presented the idea to Jerome at dinner. Jerome said he would look at it, but he could not promise that he would take the apartment. Jerome had already set his sights on an apartment in Manhattan. He would look at the Clarkson's apartment only as a favor to his parents and their new neighbors. So, he promised to stop by to meet Tasha and tour the apartment after work on the next day.

The Clarksons also presented the idea to Tasha in a phone conversation that night, however, Tasha was not happy about the idea of a strange young man living upstairs. She agreed to interview him for the possibility of taking the apartment anyway as a favor to her parents, but she wanted to make the final decision about the rental on her own. The Clarksons hoped Jerome might be the type of guy Tasha was interested in dating. They hoped their dating would turn into romance and their romance into marriage.

On the other end of the phone, you could hear the apprehension in Tasha's voice. *Here they go again with the matchmaking*, she thought. Did they not know that their set-ups never worked? Or was it just that they did not trust Tasha's judgement of a man's character? She felt her parents needed to take the training wheels off her life and finally let her ride alone. Maybe she would find her own prince in her own way and in her own time.

"So be home by 5:30 pm and have some dinner ready for your guest," Mrs. Clarkson encouraged.

"I am not making dinner for this stranger," Tasha retorted.

"Okay, Goodnight, baby."

"Bye," Tasha said before placing the phone on the hook.

Tasha did not bother to tell her mother

about her chance encounter on her long walk on Saturday. After walking a mile in Highland Park, a handsomely athletic young man bumped into Tasha while jogging and asked for advice about the bicycle trail. They talked for about ten minutes. That was long enough for her to give him a second and third thought. He gave Tasha his number after informing her of the fact that he was new to the neighborhood and had just taken a teaching position at the same elementary school where Tasha taught fourth grade. *What a coincidence,* she thought. Wondering where this chance encounter might lead gave Tasha goosebumps.

Now she had to meet with two intelligent, single, African American men who may be potential suitors. The pressure was real! What would she wear to work on Monday? Should she change clothes after school? Why was she even asking herself these questions? She was literally turning into a teenaged schoolgirl again.

Pause, girl! Wait just one minute! I'm not going down that road again, she thought. *There are no relationship goals right now. I am taking time off from that. I will not show interest in either of them.*

Then Tasha picked out the ugliest outfit she could find in her closet and laid it out to wear on Monday morning. She would be the picture of a schoolmarm. Neither David nor Jerome would be interested in her now. Her student's and colleagues would wonder what was wrong with her because she usually dressed like a modern professional teacher. This would be her inside joke and a little test for the men she was about to meet.

Sleep came easily to Tasha on Sunday evening because she was charting her own course, or so she thought. She dreamt of picking flowers in a garden and forming them into a beautifully magnificent bouquet. She awakened refreshed and rejuvenated. Tasha was more than ready to face the day.

Chapter 4

Monday morning whisked by as quickly as it came. Tasha's day was so busy at school that she only saw David for a moment in the teachers' lounge. They greeted each other briefly, and then Tasha rushed back up to her third-floor classroom. David seemed nice enough, but Tasha never mixed business with pleasure. She did not want people at her job prying into her personal life. Tasha was always a consummate professional.

With this portion of her day over, she could now concentrate on her interview with Jerome. *What would he be like?* Tasha asked herself. *Why was her mother willing to let her meet Jerome alone? What did her mother see in Jerome's parents that made her think something good could come from their DNA?* Well, Tasha was about to find out the answer to all of those questions shortly.

Tasha rushed home to get ready for the appointment. She took a shower, changed into a little black dress, and prepared a small dinner. Tasha made baked chicken, broccoli, and wild rice. She even prepared a pitcher of lemonade. For dessert, she planned to have an ice cream sundae with hot fudge on top. Afterwards, she would mark a few of her students' essays. Finally, she would curl up on the couch to read a book. Ding went the timer, and Tasha prepared her table for one again to dine alone.

Jerome did not arrive on time for his appointment that evening. He rushed to Tasha's house from an early dinner date with his girlfriend, Tonya. Tasha was already on the defensive because she believed promptness was a virtue. After all, she was a teacher. Suddenly the doorbell rang. Tasha peeked through the peephole and asked Jerome to identify himself. He recited his name, his parents' names, and his address before Tasha would even open the door.

Once inside, Jerome felt a little more at ease. He apologized for being late and explained he was on a dinner date and had lost track of time. Tasha quickly and precisely explained the terms under which she would accept Jerome as a tenant. Then she asked abruptly if he had any questions.

"I have Just one question," Jerome replied. What color are your eyes?"

Tasha laughed and said, "I meant questions you may have about the apartment business."

Jerome noticed during the entire time she spoke, she never once looked him in the eye.

Then he said, "Mother always says never trust a person who can't look you in the eye." They say the eyes are the windows to a person's emotions and I do not know how you are feeling right now."

Tasha blushed and stared directly into Jerome's eyes and said, "Do you have any questions?"

Jerome replied, "No, I will call you tomorrow to let you know if I am going to move in."

"Okay, as long as you understand the fact is if someone else answers my ad before you call, I will give them the opportunity to rent the apartment. It was very nice meeting you, Mr. Johnson."

"The pleasure was all mine," Jerome replied.

Then he disappeared through the door and stepped into his car. Tasha waved goodbye and locked the doors.

That night she thought about whether Jerome would want the apartment, now. A part of her did not care what he decided while the other part hoped he would move in. It confused Tasha. She thought about how different they were in terms of their personalities. She was a teacher, and he was about to become a lawyer. The possibility was they might never cross paths again, even if he moved in upstairs. Their work would consume all their free time, anyway. She also thought about Jerome's girlfriend visiting him if he took the apartment. Suddenly, she started feeling sick. Then, she decided it would be nice to have a man around to double as building security. With that thought in mind, she went to sleep.

While sleeping, she dreamt about Jerome walking around the courtroom in suits with a black leather briefcase pleading the cases of defendants unjustly accused by plaintiffs. She envisioned herself as a legal secretary in his office who accompanied him to court each day. When returning to the office, she would file his dockets for him in the inner office. She always wore a black suit with a tight little mini skirt every day. She would pretend to drop a paper just to bend over enough to give him a glimpse of her goodies. Afterwards, Tasha and

Jerome would go out for lunch or dinner and discuss the events of the day. In her dream, they were not a couple, but they were grand and flirtatious friends who were inseparable.

Chapter 5

The next morning, Tasha was up early cleaning and preparing for work. She changed the message on her answering machine three times before even having breakfast. She thought about how she wanted to sound if Jerome called while she was out. Tasha barely touched her breakfast; she was so nervous. Finally, she left for work.

It was a brisk October morning. Tasha noticed everything about nature that day, even though she was in a hurry. She noticed the brilliantly bright oranges and golden colors of the leaves floating down from the tree branches. As the wind kissed her face, she smiled widely, thinking of the woman she was becoming. Tasha was a young, beautiful, confident, independent, and professional African American woman. What more could she want or need for now?

Tasha picked up her class in the gymnasium that morning right on time. To her surprise, David was standing there waiting to greet her. He quickly informed her of his new position at their school. He was the new physical education teacher.

"Your class has gym today at eight period, so I'll get to see you again soon. Now, you will get to see me in my element," David said.

"I cannot wait," Tasha replied.

"See you then," David uttered before walking to inspect his supply room.

As Tasha escorted her students to their classroom, the students gossiped about Miss Clarkson's relationship with Mr. David Reed.

"Looks like Miss Clarkson has a boyfriend," Sherri snickered. "

"He's cute, too," Natasha interjected.

The rest of Tasha's class just giggled under their breaths as Miss Clarkson blushed with embarrassment.

Then Jerry stated seriously, "Miss Clarkson is a professional, so she is clearly not interested in pursuing a relationship with our new gym teacher."

On that note, Tasha asked the students

to settle down and led them up the stairs to their classroom. Once inside the room, the children focused on their work and forgot about what happened during the morning lineup. The students knew Miss Clarkson did not play about classwork and education.

However, all day long Tasha could not stop thinking about that phone call. At lunchtime, one of her colleagues gave her the name and number of another tenant who would pay even higher rent for the apartment. This tenant was a female who was around the same age as Tasha. So, Tasha told Mr. Green if Jerome did not take the apartment, her next choice would be the lady Mr. Green had suggested.

Eighth period came quickly. The students loved gym class with David that afternoon. Tasha stayed a little while to examine David's teaching style. He had a good rapport with the students. He really made each one feel special. Yet he always encouraged the students to work as a team and to show respect for others. It was a joy to see him in his element. Tasha was glad David invited her to his class.

Tasha hurried to dismiss her class on time, knowing Jerome may have left the message she was waiting for all day. When Tasha arrived home from work, she walked straight over to her answering machine. She noticed the light blinking on the base. Then Tasha immediately pressed play. The message was from her mother. Tasha's mother wanted to know if Tasha had decided on which tenant would get the apartment yet. She did not return her mother's call, because she was so eagerly awaiting Jerome's call. Tasha did not want to tie up the phone line talking to her mother.

After an hour passed, Tasha freshened up, changed her clothes, and prepared dinner. Suddenly the bell rang. Tasha walked over to the door and peeked through the peephole. To her surprise, it was Jerome standing outside. Tasha did not know how to react. *Suppose he's coming to say no to the proposition in person*, she thought.

Tasha gasped for breath. Then she opened the door slowly.

"Hi Jerome."

"Hello Tasha," Jerome replied.

"What are you doing in this part of town?"

"I just wanted to give you my answer in person, Tasha," Jerome added. "I want the apartment and I have even brought a few of my things over tonight to place in the apartment if that is alright with you. In addition, I have for you a month's security and two months rent paid in full."

"Wow! I'm amazed. Come on in."

Once inside, they chatted more warmly than they had in the past.

"I guess we will have to get to know one another better, after all we will be neighbors, now," Tasha stated.

Jerome just laughed and said, "Yeah. I guess so."

After Tasha offered Jerome a cup of coffee, she helped him carry a few of his things to the upstairs apartment. Then she gave him his keys. They said their goodbyes and Jerome drove right back to Queens. She knew he would not be back until Saturday to move into the apartment completely, but she was already missing him.

Chapter 6

On Saturday, Jerome moved his remaining belongings into his new apartment. Only this time, he brought Tonya along with him. Jerome shyly introduced Tonya to Tasha.

"Hello Tasha, Jerome has told me so much about you," Tonya said.

"Hi Tonya, nice to meet you," Tasha

replied.

Jerome seemed happy that the ladies were getting along with each other. His smile was like a hundred-watt bulb, blinding and bright. Well, at least the introduction had gone well, Tasha thought to herself.

Tonya was much more beautiful than Tasha imagined. She was intelligent and well bred, too. Tonya was the daughter of two lawyers who lived on Long Island. Therefore, Tonya also studied Law at John Jay College. Tonya lived in Manhattan to be close to her campus. When Tonya hinted she did not think it would be a good idea for Jerome to live in Brooklyn, Tasha stopped thinking so positively of her. Instead, she felt Tonya was a bit too uppity for her taste. Yet, there Tonya stood in all her glory beside Jerome, who seemed to adore her.

The lovely couple invited Tasha upstairs

for tea to celebrate Jerome's moving in day, but Tasha declined their invitation, citing she had several test papers to mark and lesson plans to complete.

Once inside her downstairs apartment, Tasha could not concentrate on her work. She kept imagining what Jerome and his girlfriend might do upstairs. At that point, she could not understand why she was so interested in Jerome's affairs. Sure, he was handsome, well educated, and kind, but he was not the only man on Earth. Tasha had to keep her options open.

Suddenly, Tasha took her mind off the new tenant. She called her friend Kathy and told her all about Jerome and Tonya before she even realized it.

Finally, Kathy interrupted by saying, "Could it be possible you feel something for Jerome?"

"Of course not," Tasha replied sharply.

"Well, if that is truly the case, why don't you go out with my brother, Kenny, tonight? He has been asking you out for months and you keep turning him down."

"Okay! I'll do it! Kathy, I will go out with Kenny. I have been meaning to contact him, anyway. I have just been so busy lately with work and all."

"Tasha, I cannot wait to hear the details when you return," Kathy said excitedly.

I'll call you back later," Tasha replied as she hung up the phone.

Next, Tasha called Kenny, and they made plans to see a movie and have dinner. Kenny planned to pick her up at 6:00 o'clock PM sharp that evening. Tasha dressed and was ready to leave by 5:30 PM. Suddenly, the doorbell rang. She opened it so quickly, only to find that it was Jerome and Tonya. Jerome explained he was about to take Tonya back home and they just wanted to say goodnight. Before Tasha could reply, Jerome noticed how beautiful she looked and asked if she was going out.

"Yes, my date will be here any minute," Tasha replied.

"Well, I'd say he's a very lucky guy," Jerome interjected before saying goodnight. Then Tasha waved goodbye to Jerome and Tonya.

As soon as Tasha closed the door, the bell rang again. This time it was Kenny.

Once inside he asked, "Who were those two people I saw leaving the building just now."

"Oh, that was my new tenant and his girlfriend."

"Well, I guess you'll feel a little safer now having a man around the house."

"I feel safe with you," Tasha replied quickly. Then they left to begin their date.

Tasha and Kenny got along very well. The film was romantic and so was the dinner. Tasha and Kenny unexpectedly were even able to engage in a lengthy stimulating, intellectual conversation on the ride back home. As Kenny walked Tasha back to the door of her downstairs apartment, they both noticed the hall light was on. The two of them felt it was a gracious gesture for the new tenant to leave the light on for Tasha. Kenny and Tasha kissed each other passionately on the lips while locked in a tight embrace before finally saying goodnight.

Once inside, Tasha jumped into her bed and thought about how romantic Kenny was. Then the doorbell rang. It was Jerome.

"Is there a problem?" Tasha asked.

"No, Jerome replied. I couldn't sleep, and I was just wondering how your date turned out."

"Well, it's kind of you to ask, however, I think that's a pretty personal question."

Then Jerome apologized and asked if he could just come in and talk for a while. Tasha said sure, and they ended up talking for two hours. Jerome joked about how Tasha's mom and dad told him to monitor their little girl for them, but she could tell that he meant it literally. After a while they felt tired, and they said their goodnights. Then Jerome headed back upstairs to his apartment.

Both Jerome and Tasha slept and dreamt restlessly that night. Jerome dreamt about Tasha instead of Tonya. Tasha dreamt about Jerome instead of Kenny. Neither Tasha nor

Jerome were fully understanding why their interests had shifted to the newest person in their lives. Their dreams just seemed so real and enjoyable. If only actual life could be as nice, they thought.

Chapter 7

The next morning Tasha hurried to get showered and dressed. She wanted to avoid seeing Jerome before heading to work that morning. Tasha did not even eat breakfast. She left her apartment an hour earlier than usual. As she sat in the parking lot before entering the school building, she thought about how incredibly childish and immature she was acting. She felt like a teenager again.

Tasha vowed to stop acting that way and to face her fears like a woman when she returned home from work that evening. After all, she was seeing Kenny now. What could develop between her and her new tenant?

A lot of things could develop according to Tasha's mom and dad. The Clarksons were getting to know the Johnsons well in their first few days in the new neighborhood. They had a lot in common. The men loved to shoot pool, read the newspaper, and watch sports on TV. While the women loved to shop at flea markets, garden, take long walks, and talk on the phone. The two retired couples talked for hours on end. Both thought it would be funny if they ended up as in-laws with their two youngest children getting to know each other in Brooklyn.

Jerome's mom, Mrs. Johnson, wanted

nothing but the best for her son, who was becoming an extremely caring attorney. She told Mrs. Clarkson how he would need a caring and supportive person on the days when he might come home after losing a case at work. Tasha's mom, Mrs. Clarkson, wanted an intelligent and caring man for her daughter who was a teacher in the city's public school system. Would they get their wish? Only time would tell if this arrangement would spark a romantic flame between their children.

"Charity Johnson, have you heard anything from your son lately?"

"Yes, Terry Clarkson. I have. He called me today at lunchtime. He wanted to tell me that your daughter went on a date last night."

"A date… A date with whom?"

"Well, he did not get the person's name, but he left the light on for your daughter so she would not have to come into a dark hall late in the evening."

"Oh, Charity, your son is such a gentleman."

"Well, if he even mentioned that Tasha had a date last night, I find to be very interesting since he has a girlfriend himself."

"You never said Jerome had a girlfriend before, Charity."

"And you never said Tasha had a boyfriend before either."

"Well, that is because she does not have a boyfriend. I don't know who took her on a date last night, but Tasha has not told me anything about it. If she did not even mention the date to me, it could only mean it was not a serious date."

"Jerome says he is going to see your daughter after work today. So, let's hope and pray they put a spark to this flame tonight."

"Okay, bye."

At that moment, Mr. Clarkson walked into the room.

"Have you been talking to Charity Johnson again?"

"Yes, husband, I have, and why does it matter to you?"

"Terry, you know I dislike you interfering with our daughter's love life."

"Love life—I wish Tasha had a love life, Mrs. Clarkson retorted. Charity and I just want what's best for our children. We cannot help it if they do not know what is best for themselves. Don't worry about us we're just two doting mothers having fun playing matchmakers for our children."

"Okay, Terry, I'm just warning you

because as you know Tasha enjoys doing things on her own," Mr. Clarkson responded.

Chapter 8

This Monday morning was hectic for Tasha. She only had lunch in the teachers' lounge for a few moments when David, the gym teacher, walked in.

"Have you been avoiding me?"

"Not at all," Tasha replied.

"I have just been terribly busy today. I had a meeting with a parent on my preparation period, so this is my first breather moment today."

"So, why don't we go for a walk today after school, Tasha? It may help you calm down after a long day at work," David suggested.

"I think I should tell you I'm seeing someone, now," Tasha stated.

"Oh, I'm happy for you, David replied. But I did not ask you out on a date. We both know I like to jog and bike at the park for exercise. We could just walk as friends and neighbors, Tasha, with no strings attached."

"Well, since you put it that way, a walk may be just what I need to clear my head. Here's my address, David. Meet me at 4:00 after school today and do not be late!"

"I promise I won't be late," David said as they hurried off to meet their students.

Tasha made it home by 3:15 pm, changed her clothes, and was ready to leave by 3:55 pm. The doorbell rang at precisely 4:00 pm. David stood outside the doorway in a green sweatsuit with green and white sneakers and a green sweatband around his head. He was ready to go. Tasha wore a black jogging suit with bright white sneakers. They took off running towards the park in silence, stopping about an hour later to sit on a bench to catch their breath.

"Wow, that was a great run! How about we pick up some bottled water from the deli near your house?"

"That would be great, David. Afterwards, I'll have to hurry home though because I have test papers to mark," Tasha stated between gasps.

So, they strolled towards the deli where they purchased two bottles of water and stood outside and drank until the bottles were empty.

"I really enjoyed myself, David," said Tasha.

"Me too, David added happily. I hope this is not the last time you decide to come and exercise with me."

"I was wondering if you had a bike. Maybe the next time we could cycle through the park."

"No, I don't have a bike and I would rather jog or run in the park, but thanks for asking anyway."

"Maybe next time we could go out for a bite to eat."

"Now David, I thought I told you I was seeing someone, so I'll have to say no to the dinner."

"Okay, but you can't blame a guy for trying."

"So, I'll see you tomorrow at school."

"Bye, Tasha."

Tasha could not wait to get home to see if Jerome had arrived home from work. She did not want David to walk her back to the house, because Jerome might see them together and get the wrong idea. Tasha hurried inside of her apartment just in time before hearing Jerome's footsteps. He came through the front door and walked upstairs to the second-floor apartment. Inside of her shower, she replayed all the images of the day in her mind, and then she even had time to add a few fanciful daydreams before coming out to dry herself off and get dressed once again. Now, she said to herself, W*hat shall I make for dinner. What am I in the mood to eat tonight?* A knock on the door interrupted her thoughts.

"Hey Tasha, it's me Jerome are you in there?"

"I'm home." Tasha replied rapidly opening the door to see Jerome standing outside. What's up?"

"Nothing important, Tasha, I was just coming to invite you and your boyfriend out to dinner with Tonya and myself this Saturday night."

"Oh, how nice! I will have to ask Kenny if he's interested in going."

"Okay, do that and let me know by tomorrow, so I can make reservations at the restaurant."

"Will do, goodnight."

"Bye," Jerome stated as he turned and walked back upstairs.

Tasha's heart was throbbing. She did not know why this occurred every time she saw Jerome. There was something about him she just could not put her finger on. And she really did not want to go out on this double date with him, but it was his call. So, she called Kenny next. She quickly picked up the phone, dialed Kenny's number, and was about to ask him how he was doing only to get his answering service. So, she left a brief message detailing the invite out on a double dinner date for Saturday night. In her message, she asked him to call her back as soon as he got in for the evening.

After having a light dinner and grading all the students' test papers, Tasha decided she would read for a while and update her calendar. However, she was unsure of what to list for Saturday evening because she had not heard from Kenny yet. So, Tasha sat on her couch and continued to read her book for at least an hour. Later, she turned on her television but could find nothing decent to watch except for the news. She focused on the news and all that was going on in the city for a half an hour. Afterward, she turned in for the evening.

As she was about to jump into the bed, her phone rang. She answered the phone, not knowing whether it could be an emergency call. So, she stepped back out from under the blanket, and picked up the phone. Whose voice was it on the other end of the line? Kenny's velvety voice awakened all her senses. Kenny was at home and returning Tasha's call.

"Hello baby," he said sensually.

"Hi, honey. Did you get my message earlier?"

"Yes, Kenny replied.

"So, you want to have a double date with the neighbor and his girl, huh?"

"Why not? I thought it was nice of him to ask us to accompany them."

"Okay, Tasha, if that's what you want to do, but sometimes I feel Jerome has a little crush on you."

"What crush? Are you kidding? He's been dating Tonya for quite some time, and they even have their vocations in common. Both are going to be attorneys at a large prestigious law firm in Manhattan. So, he could never have a crush on me."

"Okay, if you say so, Tasha, but I know what I noticed and believe me, it's a man's thing."

"A man's thing? Well, I want you to be here on Saturday at least half an hour before 6:00 pm because that is when we are leaving to go to the restaurant."

"Don't worry I'll be there, and I'll be on time. Talk to you later."

"Goodnight., Kenny."

"Goodnight, baby."

Chapter 9

The remaining days of the week flew by and before Tasha knew it, Saturday came. On Saturday, she spent her entire morning preparing for the 6:00 pm double dinner date. As she looked at herself in the mirror, she wondered why she was so anxious about going on this double date. She started thinking about all the things that had gone on in the previous weeks. She thought about her parents coincidentally meeting Jerome's parents, an accidental chance meeting with David, and her finally taking her friend up on the offer to go out with her best friend's brother. It was like a whirlwind. She could not believe that she was standing here today with a date and double dating with another man that she was slightly interested in. Yes, she was admitting to herself that she had a romantic interest in Jerome, her neighbor upstairs. Yet, she hoped it would not impede their dinner date tonight. She hoped everything would go smoothly and that she would just enjoy pleasant conversation so she could wind down from her stressful work week.

The double date started at exactly 6:00 pm. The gentlemen escorted the ladies only a few blocks away from where Jerome and Tasha lived to the local restaurant. Their neighborhood was a cultural haven, diverse and exciting, with lots of little enclaves to explore. Saturday was a lively night in their community, even in the fall. A variety of restaurants had opened up throughout the neighborhood because of ongoing gentrification. Tasha dressed in a navy blue fitted pantsuit with a short gold puffer jacket since the temperature was kind of cold that evening. She wore low-heeled shoes and stepped briskly as the cool wind whisked pass her cheeks. Kenny's embrace shielded her from being blown away by the wind. Jerome held Tonya's hand for the duration of the five-block walk to LaSalle's restaurant. Decor inside the establishment was bright yet cozy. The couples had a booth in the southeastern corner of the establishment. Service was exquisite, and the ambiance set the mood for romance. The couples dined on high-level cuisine and enjoyed intellectual conversation while jazz played in the background. They laughed and joked as they sipped their red wine. Suddenly, the ladies excused themselves from the table, saying they needed to go to the powder room. They giggled all the way there.

However, once inside, the conversation shifted. Tonya asked Tasha a series of questions. She wanted to know Tasha's background, how she met Jerome, and how she could convince him to take the apartment that she was renting above her own apartment. So, Tasha gave Tonya all the information that she asked for, but it still did not seem like it was enough for Tonya. It was as if Tonya did not believe that Jerome and Tasha could be just friends. Tonya was showing her insecurities now, although she kept suggesting to Tasha that she was sure Jerome would propose to her within the next few months. So, Tasha congratulated Tonya, and they left the powder room. Tasha bumped shoulders with a handsome young man seated at the bar on the way back to their table. When this guy turned around, she noticed it was none other than David.

David's said, "What a coincidence, Tasha! I didn't know you'd be here tonight."

So, Tasha immediately introduced Tonya to David and Tonya asked David if he would like to join their table.

David of course said, "No, I don't want to be a third wheel."

Tasha said, "At least come over and let me introduce you to the guys."

So, David walked over, and Tasha introduced him to Kenny and Jerome. David told the guys he lived in the neighborhood and worked with Tasha at the elementary school. The guys also invited David to stay, but David turned them down. He said he did not want to interrupt the lovebirds on their double date. They all laughed it off and David returned to the bar alone.

The couples then took their desserts home. The gentlemen left a large tip for the server before departing the establishment with their beautiful dates. As they walked, they chatted, and the couples embraced even more. Once at the two-story apartment, the couples parted ways. Jerome and Tonya went upstairs, and Kenny and Tasha walked into Tasha's first-floor apartment together. Tasha offered Kenny a cup of coffee to go along with his chocolate cake, and Kenny accepted the offer. They enjoyed their coffee and cake while cuddling together and whispering sweet nothings into each other's ears. "What a night," Tasha thought as she lay back on the couch.

"Can I stay with you tonight?"

Tasha was yanked back into reality with Kenny's question.

"No, Kenny I'm not ready for that kind of commitment yet."

"Okay, Tasha, I get it, Kenny responded. I realize this is only our second date, but we are moving in the right direction. It felt like we were an actual couple tonight seeing Jerome with Tonya."

"Well, Tonya and Jerome have nothing to do with our relationship, Tasha retorted. I don't even know what he sees in her," Tasha continued.

"There you go again sounding interested in Jerome! I'm leaving and I don't think I'll be coming back," Kenny said as he walked towards the door. "

Wait!"

"Bye Tasha," Kenny yelled back as he

walked out the door.

Tasha cleaned up the dishes, took a shower, and lay down in her bed. She was alone with her thoughts. Or was she just alone and destined to be a loner for the rest of her life? As Tasha thought more on the subject, she knew Kenny was right about her interest in Jerome. Tasha tried to hide those feelings, but she was not good at it at all. Her mind wondered about whether Tonya had gone home for the evening. She did not remember hearing footsteps or car doors opening and closing. "Maybe I should just mind my business," she thought as she pulled up the covers and went to sleep.

Chapter 10

Sunday after church service, Tasha went over to her parents' house in Queens. Her mom and dad were so thrilled to see her. They embraced Tasha tightly after she entered the living room. Then, they sat down and caught up in their conversation. Mrs. Clarkson wanted to know how things were going at the Brooklyn property. Tasha quickly stated things were going very well. Mr.

Clarkson commended Tasha on how well she was doing as a landlord, but Mrs. Clarkson wanted details. Knowing where the conversation between the two ladies was leading, Mr. Clarkson exited the room. He did not want to hear or take part in any gossip.

"So how are things going with Kenny?" Mrs. Clarkson asked.

"How do you know I was dating Kenny?" Tasha inquired.

"What do you mean was dating, dear?"

"Well, I went on two dates with Kenny, mom, but we ended our relationship after the second date. I felt we were moving much too fast, and Kenny felt I was interested in someone else."

"Who is this someone else, Tasha?"

"Well, just because Jerome is renting the apartment upstairs, he feels there are some feelings between Jerome and I."

Is there any truth to that, Tasha?"

"Not really, mom. Jerome is truly kind, but he has a girlfriend."

"Does this mean you are not interested in Jerome?"

"I plead the fifth amendment on that question," Tasha replied.

"Let me give you a little motherly advice, Tasha. Life is too short to let it pass you by. Sometimes we must take chances, when there is an opportunity to change our lives for the better. If you like Jerome, let him know."

"Maybe I will tell him how I feel this week," Tasha interjected.

"You will feel much better once you know how he feels."

"You are right, mom. Let's eat! I feel

better already after talking to you."

The Clarkson family dined on fried chicken, collard greens, candied sweet potatoes, and chocolate cake for dessert. Later, they watched a movie together and caught up on family gossip together. They laughed and laughed as they reminisced about Tasha's childhood days. Tasha's parents then expressed their desire to one day have grandchildren running through their house. Finally, Tasha noticed it was getting late. So, she said her goodbyes and hurried back home to Brooklyn.

Chapter 11

The Monday morning workday passed by so quickly Tasha barely said hello to David as she passed him in the hall. David seemed more distant after seeing Tasha double dating last Saturday evening. Perhaps he knew he would never ask Tasha out on an actual date now. Tasha hurried home after work, hoping to catch Jerome coming in from work himself, but she was not so lucky this time.

That night Jerome returned home late from his internship. Tasha heard him turn his key and enter the front door. She had just finished marking some of her grade four students' test papers. A full day's work had exhausted Tasha. She took a shower and turned in early. As she walked toward the bedroom, she heard a light tap at the door.

Jerome asked if he could come in and chat for a while. Tasha told him how exhausted she was and she wanted to turn him away. However, she could see the pain in his big brown eyes and she just could not turn him away. He came in and sat on her little love seat. She sat across from him in her uncle's antique chair. She did not want to chance sitting too close to him for what was only his second time in her apartment.

Tasha asked Jerome if he would like

some tea. He concurred and answered yes. Then she left him alone in the living room for 15 minutes while she prepared their tea. When she returned, he was asleep in her chair. She could not bear the thought of waking him up. He looked so cute and cuddly lying there. She sipped hot tea while watching him sleep. Then she went to take a shower and turn in for the evening.

The next morning, Tasha was up early preparing a full breakfast for Jerome and herself before work. Jerome awakened to the smells of eggs, bacon, biscuits, and hot tea. He thought he was in heaven or at his mother's house. Then he heard the sweetest sound ever floating from the kitchen. It was Tasha's voice calling him to breakfast. He was a little embarrassed that he had fallen asleep before he could talk to her last night, but he would shake off the embarrassment for a hearty breakfast with the girl of his dreams.

Yes, he was falling for Tasha. He walked into the kitchen, attending to her every word. She scolded him like a child telling him to go take a shower first. She had already prepared everything he needed to shower inside of her bathroom. However, he told her he needed to go upstairs to get his clothing and other toiletries.

He hurried back, took a quick shower, and sat down to a large breakfast and a fine conversation with a fine woman. Jerome was really enjoying his newfound friendship with Tasha. Suddenly, Tasha reminded him she had to go to work, but she promised to finish the conversation after work tonight. It delighted Jerome to concur. They each jetted off to their respective cars and zoomed off to work.

Chapter 12

Tuesday morning waltzed by slowly. Tasha felt as though she were floating on clouds. She was so in love with Jerome. Even her students and colleagues noticed a change in her demeanor. Nothing seemed to bother her on that day. She even agreed to have lunch with David in the teachers' lounge. David ordered two lunches from the school cafeteria and they ate and chatted the time away.

"So, Kenny must treat his lady well," David said, interrupting Tasha's apparent daydream.

"Not Kenny, it is Jerome who is treating me well," Tasha replied.

"Well then, give me the details," David stated with intrigue.

Tasha filled him in on the events of the previous evening, leaving nothing to his imagination. It shocked David to hear how quickly things were developing between Tasha and Jerome, especially since Jerome apparently already had a girlfriend. David felt Jerome could just be using Tasha behind Tonya's back.

David was about to tell Tasha what he thought just as the school bell sounded ending their lunch period. The two teachers ran off to pick up their classes from lunch. David worried about the possibility of Tasha getting her heart broken. He did not trust Jerome at all. David decided he would call Tasha on the phone later in the evening to give her his take on things.

When the last school bell sounded, Tasha raced out of the school building to buy groceries, hoping to cook dinner for Jerome that night. After shopping for an hour, Tasha hurried home to change clothes and start cooking. As soon as she stepped inside the doorway of her apartment, her phone rang. She placed the grocery bags on the table and answered the phone. David was on the line. He tried to talk to Tasha, but she rushed him off the phone by telling him she was busy right now. Then, Tasha washed her hands and started making dinner for two.

Two hours later, Tasha heard footsteps in the hallway. By the time Jerome arrived at her door, the door was open. He confidently stepped inside her cozy apartment and sat in his favorite spot on the loveseat, hoping Tasha would join him there tonight. And join him she did. She was wearing a pale pink satin caftan. As she sashayed into the living room, she sat down next to Jerome and asked him if he liked steak, potatoes, and string beans. He answered with a quick yes, and then they talked.

Jerome apologized for falling asleep on Tasha's couch last night. Someone had murdered an incarcerated client in a riot today, so Jerome was distraught. He said that things like that always drained him. Jerome told her how he needed someone to talk to about those things with, but his girlfriend Tonya always changed the subject. He asked Tasha if it would be alright if he talked about things sometimes with her instead. Tasha grabbed his enormous hands and said yes.

Then she hugged Jerome tightly and told him she was sure he had done all he could do for his client, because he was such a caring human being. She also told him how lucky she felt to have someone like him living upstairs.

Jerome responded by saying he was glad he moved into the upstairs apartment as well. He told Tasha he had found a true friend downstairs. Then they smiled at each other and went to the dining room table to eat dinner.

As they were eating, talking, and enjoying each other's company, Tasha's phone rang. She did not answer it right away, so the answering machine picked up the call. It was Kenny calling Tasha to ask her out on another date. Tasha hesitated a moment. Then, she picked up the phone and told Kenny that she was having dinner with Jerome tonight. So, Tasha told Kenny she would call him back later. Then, she quickly hung up the phone.

This phone call pulled both Tasha and Jerome back into reality.

Jerome asked, "Am I interfering with your relationship with Kenny?"

Tasha retorted, "No, not at all. Kenny and I have only been on two dates. So, I should ask you if you're serious with Tonya," Tasha continued.

"Well, I've dated Tonya for four years. However, we rarely even communicate in our relationship, Jerome responded. Talking to Tonya is not like talking to you."

"But four years is a long time to be in a relationship with someone, and not care about them," Tasha said.

"I did not say I didn't care about Tonya," Jerome interjected.

"Then why are you here?" Tasha yelled.

"I'm here, because I care about you," Jerome responded louder.

"You should go," Tasha said in a much softer tone.

"I don't think I should leave. Tasha, I really want to stay. I'm making my choice right here and right now, and my choice is you. This is destiny, baby. My moving upstairs helped me find you. You are my true love," Jerome said with tears in his eyes.

Tasha kissed Jerome passionately. Jerome embraced her more tightly as they sat on the love seat emblazoned in each other's love and passion. When they came up for air, they talked for two hours straight.

Finally, Jerome said, "I had better go upstairs before we go too far too fast."

Tasha agreed, although she really did not

want him to leave.

Chapter 13

Everything fell into place like the pieces of a scenic jigsaw puzzle, except one little puzzle piece did not fit. How was Jerome going to tell Tonya about his sudden change of mind? How do you just break up with someone after four years? There is so much history between people in a committed relationship. How do you just throw all that history away?

Jerome wrestled with the scenarios of ways he could tell Tonya it was over between them. *Maybe I can just take her out to lunch and have that conversation with her,* he thought. Jerome called Tonya to schedule a lunch date on Thursday. Tonya agreed to meet him at noon at their favorite pizza spot in Manhattan.

When Thursday arrived, Jerome was nervous all day. He really did not know what to say. The seasoned, eloquent attorney he was about to become had vanished. All that remained was a babbling buffoon of a boy in a handsome man's body. He breathed hard and his palms were sweaty as he waited at their special booth— waiting for the two gourmet thin crust pizzas.

Tonya asked upon her arrival, "What's wrong, Jay?"

She could read him like a book. After all,

they had dated for four years straight. By now, they were best friends who behaved more like a married couple. When Jerome avoided her question, Tonya knew something was seriously wrong. Just then the server came over to the table to serve their pizzas and drinks. Tonya sat down quickly and insisted Jerome tell her what was going on.

Jerome stuttered, but Tonya cut him off before he could speak.

"This is about your new landlord, isn't it, Jerome?"

"Yes," Jerome responded.

"I saw this coming," Tonya retorted.

"I knew Tasha was after you the first time I saw her," Tonya continued. "So, you have succumbed to her beguiling advances," Tasha yelled.

"No, the feelings were mutual, Tonya. I

am so sorry," Jerome added as Tonya stood up with tears in her eyes.

"Well, I am not sorry," Tonya responded. "I am just done with you!"

Tonya dashed out of the pizza shop in a rage. Jerome did not bother to chase her. He just sat there embarrassed while eating two pizzas instead of one. He left a decent tip before exiting the restaurant himself.

It was an exceptionally long afternoon at his internship. Jerome could not wait to get home to tell Tasha what had occurred at the restaurant. He hoped Tasha would have dinner waiting. He was not in the mood for take-out or for ordering in fast food. Jerome loved the fact that Tasha could cook. Tasha reminded Jerome a lot of his mother. He was sure Tasha would bond easily with his family. Tasha was not uppity like Tonya. Jerome filed the last pages of a case his boss was working on and hurried out of the office as he thought of how happy Tasha would be to see him.

Chapter 14

What Jerome did not know was Tonya did not go back to her job after lunch, instead Tonya went to pay Tasha a visit. When Tasha arrived home at 3:30 pm, it surprised her to see Tonya standing at the front door of her apartment house. Tasha walked right up to Tonya to say hello. Tasha quickly told Tonya that Jerome would probably still be at work.

Tonya replied by saying, "Hello Jezebel!"

From Tonya's response, Tasha figured Tonya had already met with Jerome and knew he was no longer Tonya's man.

Tasha tried to reason with Tonya, but Tonya was not having it. At that moment, David came jogging by. He noticed the two women were arguing and played the role of a good Samaritan. David told the ladies to calm down and consider the idea that maybe Jerome is not good enough for either of them. He told them they had forgotten who they were, and no man is worth that. That statement extinguished the fiery argument, causing both ladies to apologize. Tonya then left, promising to never return to that house again.

Tasha thanked David for bringing her back to her right mind. David told her it was okay because we are all human.

"Good luck with your new relationship, Tasha."David stated.

Then took off running in route to Highland Park. Tasha waved goodbye and abruptly entered her home.

Tasha was glad Jerome had not yet arrived home from work. She felt like a fool and wondered if Jerome was the right man for her. Tasha called her mother for advice. The phone rang out three times before her mother answered the call, and hearing Tasha's voice on the other end of the phone, surprised Mrs. Clarkson.

After explaining the events of the day, Tasha began crying. Mrs. Clarkson knew it was not normal for Tasha to be so emotional about things.

"You must really like Jerome," Mrs. Clarkson whispered softly.

"I do, mom," Tasha replied through her tears.

"If you love him, then you must fight for him, Tasha. You should feel better now that your feelings are out in the open. Tonya will get over her loss and move on just as you have in the past. All of you are still young. You have so much to learn about life and relationships. Now try to get some rest this afternoon," Mrs. Clarkson said as she ended the call.

Chapter 15

When Jerome walked in, he could smell the aroma of delicious food emanating from Tasha's apartment. One tap on the door and Tasha opened the door to the next chapter in her life. At dinner they discussed the events of the day like two mature adults. Each of them felt bad about Tonya's feelings being hurt, but they agreed it was better to be truthful and just rip the bandage off the wound of their relationships so that the healing could begin.

Each of them retired to their own apartments that evening to gain more clarity on the situation. Jerome had to study for the pending bar exam and Tasha had tests to grade. Both worked through the late hours of the night, falling asleep on their couches.

Tasha awakened confused about where she was after a nightmare. She dreamt Jerome was still seeing Tonya behind her back. In the dream, she came home early from work and found them together. She felt so insecure in the dream. This dream really disturbed her.

Before she knew it, it was time to take a shower and get ready for work. Jerome tapped on the door and brought her a cup of tea. He kissed her on her forehead and held her hand. Then he asked if he could come in and chat for a while. Tasha let him in reluctantly. They shared their schedules for the day and promised to go out to dinner after work. Both needed a break after their tumultuous week.

They kissed on the lips and hurried off to work. Each of them was thinking about how they would build this relationship from here on. The relationship work was just beginning. Would they weather the storm? Maybe it would work. At least they had the support of their families.

Tasha's mother had given her powerful advice on how to proceed, and Mrs. Johnson was cheering for them as well. Mrs. Johnson told Tasha's mom that Tonya was too uppity for her taste. Mrs. Johnson wanted a down-to-earth wife for her son. Tasha had not yet met Mrs. Johnson; however, Tasha's mother had become a fast friend with Mrs. Johnson. With things moving as quickly as they were with Tasha and Jerome, Tasha knew she would meet Jerome's parents soon.

Chapter 16

At school, David was sure to stop by Tasha's classroom to find out if she was okay after the argument with Tonya yesterday. Tasha flashed the okay hand signal and David knew not to worry about her anymore. David and Tasha ate lunch together later in the day. They were in the middle of cracking another joke when a delivery person arrived with flowers for Tasha.

The red rose and baby's breath arrangement was huge. Everyone gathered around to find out who the flowers were from. The card had a loving message from Jerome. In the message, he stated he could not wait to see her tonight. The colleagues were so happy for Tasha to be getting the treatment she deserved. The students, the staff, and the administration loved her.

The bell rang, signaling the end of lunchtime. David, Tasha, and her colleagues all raced back to their posts. Once inside of her classroom, Tasha's students started giggling and chanting Mrs. Clarkson's got a boyfriend. Tasha asked the children to quiet down, and they complied.

However, one student yelled out, "Mrs. Clarkson's boyfriend is our gym teacher, Mr. David Reed."

Tasha quickly told the class that Mr. Reed

was not her boyfriend.

"We are just colleagues," Tasha said loudly. "And these flowers are not from Mr. Reed, so let us get back to work."

The students finished their day more quietly, but they seemed disappointed that Mr. David Reed was not dating Tasha.

In retrospect, Tasha knew David Reed was a good, kind, and chivalrous man. She just never thought of him as more than a friend, because she was so busy with Jerome, Kenny, and with working. Maybe she was missing David's subtle advances. Or maybe David was just a being a good friend and colleague. It did not even matter now, because she was with Jerome now.

When the last school bell sounded, Tasha rushed home to see her man. He arrived home by 4:00 pm and they were ready to go out to dinner by 6:00 pm.

This time they dined in Manhattan. After dinner, Jerome surprised Tasha with tickets to a Broadway show. Jerome was really scoring points tonight. Tasha was so enamored with Jerome that she could not think straight. A smile stayed on her face all night. After the show, Tasha and Jerome strolled down the streets of Manhattan for a brisk walk. They talked about everything as they held hands, taking in all the sights. Tasha and Jerome were inseparable after that night.

Chapter 17

The evening Tasha and Jerome spent in Manhattan led to many more romantic dates. They attended movies, office parties, sports events, and family gatherings. Everyone they met admired their relationship. However, sometimes Tasha worried about Tonya. Knowing she was the reason Tonya and Jerome ended their four-year relationship, bothered Tasha a little. However, Jerome always reassured Tasha that he and Tonya would have never made it in a long-term relationship or a marriage because Tonya wanted to control every aspect of his life. Still, Tasha had to come to terms with her feelings about what had occurred between her and Tonya.

Then there were days when Tasha thought about how David was a genuine friend through all the drama that had transpired. She wondered secretly if she was choosing the wrong partner for life. Tasha knew David was romantically interested in her and he was a good neighbor, too. At school, David was hardworking and professional. The students loved him. Tasha knew David would one day become a good father because he was already an exceptional role model for his students.

There were also times when Jerome even questioned Tasha's relationship with David. Jerome did not believe women and men could have platonic relationships. So, Jerome often accompanied David and Tasha on jogging and exercise days. Tasha felt Jerome was feeling insecure in their relationship whenever he expressed those views about David. Yet, Tasha thought Jerome's being jealous of her friendship with David was cute. Tasha wanted Jerome to show interest in her daily activities. *And to think all of this had transpired in one year because I needed a neighbor or someone to rent the upstairs apartment to,* Tasha thought.

Chapter 18

The ending of their past relationships fertilized their newfound love. Jerome continued with his internship until he passed the bar exam and became a partner at his firm, and Tasha continued teaching grade four in the public school system. David Reed remained friends with both Tasha and Jerome. In fact, they all jog together in Highland Park for exercise when the weather permits.

Jerome and Tasha's parents remained grand friends and eventually became close in-laws and grandparents. Jerome and Tasha married a year later in spring and sold the two-family apartment house in Brooklyn. They moved into a one family home in Queens, New York, just one block away from their parents. Tasha and Jerome often sat around the dinner table on holidays each year after that, talking about how they met while he was living upstairs, and she was living downstairs. They no longer need a neighbor now because love surrounds them on all sides. For Tasha Clarkson-Johnson, her neighbor has become a lifelong companion, lover, partner, and friend.

TO MY READERS

Thanks so much for reading my book. I hope you enjoyed it.

If you would like to submit a review of my books on Amazon, or other places where my books are sold feel free to do so at the following places online.

www.amazon.com

books2read.com/neighborneeded

teresawhitakersbooks.wordpress.com

teesblog.video.blog

Sincerely,

Teresa Whitaker

teestalktime1@gmail.com

ABOUT THE AUTHOR

Teresa Whitaker is a retired New York City Public School teacher, an app developer, a blogger, and a podcast host. Neighbor Needed is her first novella. She currently lives in Brooklyn, New York.

www.ingramcontent.com/pod-product-compliance
Lightning Source LLC
LaVergne TN
LVHW020643100826
845148LV00012B/2310